Born to Be Wild

THE WEEBIE ZONE #3

Born to Be WILD

by Stephanie Spinner and Ellen Weiss

illustrated by Steve Björkman

HarperCollins*Publishers*

Born to Be Wild
Text copyright © 1997 by Stephanie Spinner and Ellen Weiss
Illustrations copyright © 1997 by Steve Björkman
For information address HarperCollins Children's Books, a division of HarperCollins Publishers, 10 East 53rd Street, New York, NY 10022.

Library of Congress Cataloging-in-Publication Data
Spinner, Stephanie.
  Born to be wild / by Stephanie Spinner and Ellen Weiss ; illustrated by Steve Björkman.
    p.   cm. — (Weebie zone ; #3)
  Summary: A boy who can talk to animals and his pet gerbil team up to reunite a runaway bunny with its distraught owner.
  ISBN 0-06-027338-0 (lib. bdg.). — ISBN 0-06-442033-7 (pbk.)
  [1. Human-animal communication—Fiction. 2. Rabbits—Fiction.
3. Pets—Fiction. 4. Animals—Fiction.] I. Weiss, Ellen, date. II. Title.
III. Series: Spinner, Stephanie. Weebie zone ; #3.
PZ7.S7567Bo   1997   96-13687
[Fic]—dc20   CIP
                                                                   AC
```
          1  2  3  4  5  6  7  8  9  10
                       ❖
                  First Edition
```

For Karina
—S.S.

For Kristi
—S.B.

Contents

....

Hasta la Vista, Joanie

"Yeeowww! Yeeowww! Yeeowwrrr!"

Loud, unhappy wails were coming from the back of the Hunter family station wagon. They were being produced by Joan, the family cat.

"Joan, really," said Mrs. Hunter. "Why are you fussing? Last time you went to Pet Paradise, you liked it a lot. Remember?"

"Liked it a lot?" meowed Joan. She was in her carrier on the backseat, next to Garth Hunter, who was nine years old. "I'd rather eat mothballs for breakfast than go back to that place."

1

"Poor baby," soothed Mrs. Hunter. "Maybe you're just carsick."

"Not," growled her cat.

Mrs. Hunter didn't know what Joan was saying. But Garth knew. So did Garth's gerbil, Weebie. They understood every word. But Garth wasn't going to tell his mother that. He'd thought it over. And he was sure it was a bad idea.

How could anyone—even his mother—believe what had happened just a short time ago? He could hardly believe it himself. Yet it was true. One day Weebie, the class gerbil, had bitten him. And from then on Garth could understand what Weebie was saying. Not only that, he could understand other animals, too. Like Joan.

Garth could just imagine trying to tell his parents. They'd exchange looks and try to smile. Then they'd send him straight to a child psychologist, who'd have him play with stuffed animals.

"Tell me everything the little animals are

saying to you," the psychologist would say kindly.

Garth didn't want this to happen. He had nothing against psychologists—his mother was a psychologist—but he hated the thought of people thinking he was really, truly crazy. So he kept quiet about understanding animals. Which wasn't always so easy.

It sure wasn't easy now.

Joan was yowling her head off in her carrier, and it was about as much fun as listening to a broken car alarm. "I don't want to go to that place!" she yowled. "Garth! Weebie! Don't let her take me there! I hate it!"

"What's so bad about it?" asked Weebie, from Garth's shirt pocket. Weebie was much more relaxed about talking to Joan when she was in her carrier. That way there was almost no chance that she'd eat him.

"You'll see," she moaned.

A few minutes later they pulled into the driveway of Pet Paradise.

"You'll be fine here," Mrs. Hunter said to

Joan. "And it's only a little over a week, puss."

Garth hauled the carrier out of the car and followed his mother inside. A plump woman in a pink dress at the front desk greeted them.

"Why, this must be Joan!" she exclaimed. "Come in! Her apartment is all ready for her!"

"Apartment?" squeaked Weebie. "What *is* this place, anyhow?"

While his mother filled out papers, Garth looked around the office. The walls were covered with postcards from faraway places. He read one.

"Dear Fluffy," it said. "Barbados is grand, but we miss you, angel-kitty! We know you'll be good and clean your plate every day. And you won't scratch anyone, will you?

"Much love and a great big kiss from Mommy and Daddy."

"Angel-kitty!" muttered Garth. "Unbelievable!"

His mother finished signing papers, and it was time to get Joan settled. The woman led them out of the office and down a hallway

decorated with paintings of palm trees and beaches. There were smaller hallways off the main one, with signs saying "Hawaii" and "Bermuda" and "Miami." The woman led them down a hallway marked "Mexico."

"Joan will be staying here while you're away," she told them. "In one of our kitty condos." She led them into a long room lined with cages. Soft violin music was playing, and there was a sweet flowery smell in the air.

"If you like, we can put a television in her apartment," said the woman, "for a small extra charge." She smiled brightly. "Some boarders actually watch the soaps!" she told them.

"Ahh . . . I don't think so," said Mrs. Hunter. She wasn't a big fan of television for humans, much less animals.

"Of course the music that's piped in is free," the woman added.

"I think I'm going to throw up," said Joan.

"Poor Joan," said Mrs. Hunter, patting the carrier. "I wish we could take you to Maine, but we can't. Our landlady's allergic—she made us

6

promise to board you. But you'll be fine here. I know you will."

"Here we are," said the woman. "Four D." She opened the wire-mesh door of one of the cages. Inside was the living room of a special cat-sized apartment.

A little armchair, just big enough for a cat to curl up in, sat next to a fake fireplace painted with flames. Opposite the chair was a big carpet-covered scratching post. The pink walls were hung with postcards of sunny beaches. A small doorway led to a bathroom, which contained a bright-pink litter box.

"Gag me," whined Joan.

"Every cat goes outside for an hour a day," said the woman. "We make sure they get enough exercise."

"This is a high-class prison!" Joan meowed.

"I wonder if there are ever riots," said Weebie.

Mrs. Hunter scratched Joan behind the ears and gave her a last kiss on the head. "We'll be back before you know it," she said.

Joan stepped into her apartment. "I'll know it," she said. "Trust me."

The woman in pink escorted them out. "Don't forget to send Joan a postcard!" she called gaily as they got into the car.

Into the Woods

Garth's parents wanted to travel to Maine on Friday evening. That way they'd wake up in their vacation house on Saturday. So as soon as Mr. Hunter got home from work, they set off.

By the time they were on the highway going north, it was dark. Mr. Hunter was driving, staring straight at the road. Mrs. Hunter, next to him, kept nodding off. Whenever oncoming headlights shone into their car, she'd jerk awake and apologize. "Sorry, honey," she'd say sleepily. "I'll keep you company, I promise."

At about nine o'clock she turned around and said, "Hey, Garth, how about a game of geography?"

But she was too late. Garth was curled up in the backseat of the station wagon, asleep. Weebie was nestled in the crook of Garth's arm. He was sleeping too.

A few hours later Garth heard his mother calling his name. "Garth, here we are, sweetie," she said, stroking his hair.

He struggled to open his eyes. "Where are we? What time is it?"

"We're in Maine, at the cabin," his mother told him. "It's about twelve thirty."

Garth rubbed his eyes and climbed out of the car. "Hey!" A squeaky, sleepy little voice stopped him. "What about me?"

"Oh, sorry, Weeb," said Garth. He reached into the car and put Weebie into his pocket. Weebie immediately curled up and went back to sleep.

There was a short path between the trees

from the car to the cabin. Garth's father led the way with a flashlight. It was a cool night. The only sounds were the wind rustling the leaves and Garth's father, talking to himself as they climbed the porch steps. "Have to find the key," he mumbled, bending down. "Under the flowerpots. To the left of the door? To the right of the door? Ah! Here it is."

He poked around under a stack of flower-pots, stood with a key in his hand, and unlocked the door. It swung open.

"Whew!" said Garth's mother. "What's that smell?"

Garth stepped in as his father fumbled for the light switch. "Pee-yew!" he said. "I think something died in here."

Weebie stuck his nose out of Garth's pocket, sniffed once, and retreated quickly.

There was a click, and the lights flick-ered on.

"Hmmm," said Garth's father as he looked around.

"Well," said his mother, "it's . . . cozy."

Garth saw that the kitchen and living room were one big room. The linoleum kitchen floor was a strange design—like brick, but with grass growing between the bricks. The refrigerator and stove were both green, and there was a calendar on the wall from Ed's Garage: "The Pride of Pawtucket."

The cabin walls were covered with pine paneling, spotted with big round black knots. Green carpeting covered the floors. It was spotted too, with big brown stains. A sofa and two easy chairs wore rumpled slipcovers of some brown flowered material.

Garth's father opened a window. "Let's air the place out a little," he said.

"I think I'll go to sleep," said Garth.

"Good idea," said his mother. "Let's find the bedrooms."

The two bedrooms were just off the main room. Garth chose the smaller one, with cowboys-and-Indians curtains. He was so sleepy, he didn't care much about anything but falling into bed.

He pulled off his clothes, set Weebie down next to his pillow, and was asleep before his mother had turned off the light.

Meanwhile, not far away, a little white bunny with a big blue bow tied around his neck was hopping through the woods. He wasn't used to being outside, but anything was better than where he had been before.

"Hey, you guys!" he called out, panting a little. "Hey! Wait up!" He was trying to catch up to the band of wild rabbits who were bounding through the forest ahead of him. But he was having a very hard time. The rabbits were going really fast. The bunny had never been in a forest before, and he kept tripping over fallen branches and tree roots. Worse, the dark was beginning to scare him.

"Try a little harder," the leader of the wild rabbits called back to him. "Remember—no pain, no gain." The other rabbits snickered and ran a little faster.

The bunny with the bow tried to speed up,

and the little metal heart attached to his bow jingled in the night. "Ding Dong" was engraved on the heart. For that was his name: Ding Dong.

"We warned you about running away from home," called the leader. "We told you it would be tough. But you wouldn't listen, would you? You had to find out the hard way—little pet bunnies don't belong with real rabbits. Little pet bunny-wunnies can't do the WILD RABBIT DANCE!"

This was the rabbits' cue to break into a mad, thumping dance. A lot of them were laughing.

"Bunnies can't run with the rabbits!" sang the leader. "Bunnies don't have what it takes!" The other rabbits chanted along, thumping in rhythm. "Bunnies aren't born to be wild!"

Ding Dong sat there panting, his heart heavy. For weeks he had watched the wild rabbits. For weeks he had longed to join in their wild rabbit dances. Every night he had dreamed of being free, just like them.

Ding Dong had never been free. He was a

pet bunny, owned by an eight-year-old girl named Abigail. Abigail loved Ding Dong, but she treated him like a doll. She picked him up every two minutes. She dressed him in doll clothes. She wheeled him around in a doll carriage and tied bows around his neck. She even talked baby talk to him.

Sometimes the wild rabbits would come to the window of Abigail's cabin. They would watch her play with Ding Dong and they would laugh. This made him feel terrible. Soon he began to dream about running away, of being free and wild.

Then, last night, he had gotten his chance. Someone had left the cabin door open. Nobody was watching. So Ding Dong hopped out the door and set off to find his wild cousins in the forest.

But now he knew. His cousins were not nice. They were not nice at all.

Owner Heartbrocken

The next morning Garth woke up to the smell of pancakes. He swung his feet to the floor, yawned, and stretched. Beside him Weebie yawned and stretched too.

"Come and get 'em!" called his mother from the kitchen. "Pancakes made with Maine blueberries, piping hot!"

"Mmmm," said Weebie. "Let's go."

With Weebie in his pajama pocket, Garth stumbled out into the living room. The place didn't look so bad in daylight. And the awful smell was almost gone.

His father was setting the table, so Garth helped. There were orange plastic plates, yellow plastic glasses, and clear plastic forks and spoons. For some reason there was only one knife. The tablecloth, also plastic, had a large hole burned in it.

But the pancakes were great. "Where'd these blueberries come from?" Garth asked. He held Weebie in his palm and gave him a little piece of pancake to munch on.

"I went out this morning and bought them at a farm stand," said his mother. "It's beautiful around here. The lake is just gorgeous."

"Did you see any kids?" asked Garth.

"No, come to think of it. I didn't."

"Maybe you'd like to take a walk after breakfast," suggested Mr. Hunter. "See if you can find some."

"Okay," said Garth.

So after breakfast he put on his sneakers, put Weebie in his shirt pocket, and set out to find some kids.

He took the lake road, and as he walked

along, he realized his mother was right—it *was* beautiful here. The sky was deep blue, without a single cloud in it. The air smelled great— fresh and green. Sunlight sparkled and danced on the lake, which was just the right size, thought Garth—not too big to swim across, but big enough for a canoe.

There were cabins all around the lake, just like the one he and his parents were in. Many sat under huge pine trees. Quite a few seemed empty.

The first one he passed had its windows boarded up. So did the one after that. But the third house had people in it. A couple walked near the water's edge. An old couple.

The woman waved. "Nice to see a youngster around here," she called to him.

Uh-oh, thought Garth. Was he the only kid?

At the next house a man was unloading his station wagon. He was pulling out plastic lounge chairs, golf clubs, and a butterfly net. His hair, Garth saw, was white.

"Hello, young man," he said when he saw Garth.

"Hi," said Garth, forcing a smile.

After that he came to a big cabin that looked like it was for recreation. There were Ping-Pong tables and a knock-hockey set inside, along with four old people playing cards.

"Hi, there, youngster," said one of the women.

"Hi," said Garth, backing out of the doorway quickly.

At the next house a couple in bathing suits who looked about eighty years old were putting on white rubber bathing caps.

They smiled and waved. Garth decided to turn around.

"Gosh," said Weebie. "The place isn't exactly crawling with young folk, is it?"

"This is going to be some weird vacation," said Garth. By the time he got back to his cabin, he was feeling pretty bad.

"How was your walk?" asked his mother when she heard him come in.

"Stupid," he told her. "There aren't any kids here. Everybody's old."

"How old?"

"Like forty. At *least*."

Garth's parents looked at each other and laughed. He hated when they did that.

"Would you cut it out?" he asked.

"Sorry," said his mother, trying not to smile. "It's just that—well, I guess *we're* old, then."

This didn't make sense to Garth. He never thought of his parents as old.

"Tell you what, pal," said Garth's father. "We passed a little general store on the way in last night. Why don't we drive over there and see if they know any kids on the lake?"

"Great idea," said his mother. "Pick something up for dinner while you're at it, okay?"

So half an hour later Garth and his father drove to the store. Garth got to ride in the front seat, which he liked. Most of the time it was the backseat for him.

And since Garth was alone with his dad, Weebie got to ride on the dashboard. He faced front and looked out the windshield.

"Hey, great view from up here!" he squeaked. "Wow! We're going really fast!" They were going about fifteen miles an hour. "Hey! Look out! Watch that pothole in the road! Yikes! We're getting too close to the trees! You're driving like a maniac!"

"Squeaky little devil, isn't he?" said Garth's father. "I wonder what he's making all that noise about."

Garth just smiled.

"Sometimes," said his father, "I think it would be so incredible if we could actually talk to them. If we knew what they were saying."

"Yeah," said Garth.

"I mean, I'll bet they're really wise," said Garth's father. "I'll bet they could teach us a lot."

"Are we there yet?" squeaked Weebie.

Deep in the woods Ding Dong had finally stopped to rest. He was tired, so tired he'd stopped caring about finding something to eat or catching up with the wild rabbits. He huddled up at the base of a big tree and closed his eyes.

An instant later they flew open. He had just remembered about the snakes.

And that was the end of naptime for Ding Dong.

Garth liked the general store. It was dark and cool, and its wooden floor was sprinkled with sawdust. There were pots and pans, candles, hurricane lamps, and a pickle barrel. There were little plastic toys in yellowed plastic bags that looked as if they'd been there for a hundred years.

On the counter, next to a giant brass cash register, were jars of candy. Sugar babies. Red devils. Candy dots on long paper. Leaves made out of maple sugar. Garth's father bought him a leaf, and it melted in his mouth.

While Garth looked around, his father talked to the storekeeper. He was old (*really* old) and wore a long white apron.

"Can't say's I know of any kids around here," said the man, stroking his chin. "Nope. It's just the summer people now, and they change all the time. Why don't you take a look at the bulletin board?" He pointed to the entrance. "Might be something on it."

Garth and his father started reading the notices that were tacked on the board. Bait for sale. Boat for sale. House for rent. Car for sale. Handyman.

"What's this?" said Garth's father. A note written in crayon was tacked to the bottom of the board. It was definitely a kid's handwriting, thought Garth.

LOST RABBIT. WHITE.
NAME TAG SAYS DING DONG.
OWNER HEARTBROCKEN.
PLEASE CALL 555-8691.

"That's a kid, all right," said Mr. Hunter. "Let's take the number down." They borrowed a pen from the storekeeper, and Garth wrote the number on his finger.

On the drive home he felt a lot more cheerful. Judging by the handwriting, the kid was probably the same age as Garth. Maybe they could play knock-hockey together.

Vacation was definitely improving.

CHAPTER FOUR

Ding Dong
in Danger

When they got home, they told Mrs. Hunter the good news.

"That's great!" she said to Garth. "I hope he's nice. Do you want to call the number, or do you want me to do it?"

Garth thought his mother should do it. He always got kind of shy on the telephone.

She dialed the number. "Hello?" she said. "Is this the home with the lost rabbit?"

Garth could hear the buzz of a voice on the other end. It was a grown-up.

"Oh, no," said his mother. "I didn't mean to

get your hopes up—we didn't find your rabbit."
Then she explained that she had a son who was
looking for someone to play with.

There was more buzzing from the other
end.

"Ohhh," said Mrs. Hunter slowly. Her
expression changed. "I see. Well, maybe they'd
still like to get together. You never know." She
sounded dubious.

Garth heard more buzzing. What was going
on?

"Okay!" said his mother. "Tomorrow after-
noon it is. Number sixty-two. Got it." Then she
said good-bye and hung up.

When she turned to Garth, there was a
funny smile on her face. "I don't know why you
assumed it was a *boy* who lost a rabbit," she
said.

"Oh, *no!*" howled Garth. "You mean I have
to play with a *girl*?!"

As night fell, Ding Dong found himself
almost missing the wild rabbits. They were

mean, but at least they were company.

It was lonely out here by himself, and every noise, however soft, made him quake with fear.

The moon rose, casting its pale light onto the ground. Ding Dong heard a rustling noise. What could it be? Trembling, he peeked around.

"Excuse me—can I help you?"

Ding Dong's eyesight wasn't very good. He squinted out into the trees.

"Over here," said the gentle voice. Ding Dong looked harder. A deer, half hidden in the pines, stepped into a patch of moonlight. She had a dappled fawn with her.

"I hope you don't mind my saying so," said the deer, "but this is not such a good neighborhood for you. You really ought to think about going back to where you came from."

"Yeah," said the fawn in a bratty voice. "You better go home. You're in big trouble."

"I would go home," said Ding Dong miserably, "if I could." As bad as Abigail was, he would gladly put up with her now. She could put *pink* ribbons on him—all he wanted was to be safe again.

"So why can't you go home?" asked the fawn.

"I'm lost!" Ding Dong bawled.

"Oh, dear, oh, dear," said the deer, her big brown eyes full of sympathy. "I'm sure you'll find your way back soon." A look of concern crossed her face. "Though it's probably better to set off in daylight."

"Why?" asked Ding Dong.

"Because of the owls."

At that very moment a soft *who who who WHOOO* could be heard from above.

"The owls?" asked Ding Dong. "What do they do?"

"They eat bunnies!" said the fawn gleefully.

"Shush, dear," said the deer.

Now Ding Dong was really scared.

"You'll be all right," the deer assured him. "Just find some shelter for a while. They only hunt at night, you know. They sleep during the day.

"If you do travel, stay under cover," she added. "That way they may not see you from above."

Ding Dong was a pure, creamy white—not the best color for blending in with the forest, he knew.

"Oh, and don't eat those purple berries," added the deer as she moved back among the trees with her fawn. "They're poison."

For many long moments after the deer left, Ding Dong stayed where he was, huddled on the ground. He was so frightened, he couldn't move. But how could he stay here, out in the open? He'd never get to safety that way.

Desperately, he hopped toward the trees. And there, right in front of him, was a tree stump with a hole in it just big enough for one small creamy-white bunny.

Ding Dong scrambled inside and crouched there, panting. Maybe, just maybe he'd be safe. After all, the opening in the stump was so small, the owls would have a hard time getting him out.

They might not even see him.

"*Whooo?*" said a voice right above him. "Whooo do we have here? Can it be a *bunny?*"

"I do believe it is," said another voice. "A plump little white bunny." Ding Dong squelched a sob of pure misery. He closed his eyes. Maybe if he kept them closed long enough, the voices would go away.

"What's a nice little bunny like you doing out in the big woods all by yourself?" asked the first voice.

"Baaaaad neighborhood for bunnies," said the second voice. "Very, *very* bad."

Ding Dong opened his eyes. They weren't going away. He forced himself to look up.

In the pine tree above him were three great big brown owls. They had yellow eyes as big as dinner plates and sharp, hooked beaks. And they were all looking straight at him.

CHAPTER FIVE

Owl Be
Seeing You

"**W**anna play with us?" asked one of the owls. "We know some really good games, don't we, guys?" The other owls snickered.

"Our favorite game is called pat the bunny," cackled the third owl. "Wanna see how we play it?" All three of them hooted mirthfully.

Ding Dong kept silent. What could he say? Please don't eat me?

"I think we need to get to know this bunny," said the first owl. "I think he's a very special bunny." He flew down to a lower branch.

"A very *delicious* bunny," said the third owl, flying down to join him.

"Don't be crude," said the second owl. He flew closer too. Now they were all within a few feet of Ding Dong. They looked huge.

Ding Dong, frozen with dread, thought longingly of Abigail. So what if she dressed him in a tutu? So what if she gave him a silly name? At least she was trying to be nice to him, in her way.

Not like these . . . creatures, who kept making horrible jokes about bunny snacks. Hooting and screeching, they slapped each other with their wings when one of them said something especially funny.

Sooner or later, thought Ding Dong, they'd get tired of making jokes. Then they'd swoop down and—

It was too awful to think about.

But as time went on, and the owls stayed on their branch, Ding Dong realized they weren't coming any closer. He wondered why. Was it because they couldn't really get at him while he cowered inside the tree stump? Were they waiting for him to make a run for it?

Let them wait, thought Ding Dong. He wasn't moving.

Just as he decided this, he noticed that the owls' feathers weren't just brown, as he'd first thought. No. They were a mixture of many colors—brown, gray, and black. He could see them much more clearly now.

The little rabbit's ears shot up. He could see the owls better because the night was ending! The sky, once black, was now silvery gray. What was it the deer had said? That owls only hunted in the nighttime?

Yes! They slept during the day!

This was the thought that gave Ding Dong strength as the sky brightened and the owls began to get drowsy.

"You know what we're called?" the leader asked Ding Dong. "I'll bet you don't. Well, I'll tell you. We're called the Fly-by-Nights. We're famous all over the forest. Nobody messes with us." He blinked. His big yellow eyes looked a little glazed.

"Yeah," said the second owl. "We're rough." He blinked too.

"And tough," added the third owl. He blinked and began leaning toward the second owl. Slowly, like window shades coming down, his lids shut. As his eyes closed, he leaned farther and farther toward his friend.

"Hey!" screeched the second owl as the third owl landed on him. "Wake up!"

"Oh. Right." The third owl's eyes flew open.

"Yeah," said the first owl slowly. "We have stuff to do here. We . . . have to . . . eat . . ."— now his eyes were closing too—". . . this . . . um, this . . ."

"Bunny," finished the second owl, as the first fell asleep.

Ding Dong held his breath. As soon as their eyes were closed, he decided, he would run for his life.

Ten minutes later it finally happened. After half drifting off to sleep, jerking awake, and muttering, all the Fly-by-Nights had closed their eyes.

They were asleep.

Very, very carefully, Ding Dong climbed out of his tree stump. As silently as he could, he hopped away toward the trees. Then, when the owls were only three dark smudges on a faraway branch, he began to run.

He zoomed through the woods as fast as the opening pitch in a series game, with only one thing on his mind—to get away from those big bad birds before they woke up.

Then something wonderful happened. Ding Dong saw a cabin—a cabin with a front porch. He felt so happy and relieved that he hopped straight up into the air. He was home!

All he had to do was hop across a clearing and he'd be there. He crouched under a bush, breathing hard, and gathered his strength. Then he took off.

Halfway to the cabin he heard a terrifying sound: the flapping of wings. Owl wings.

He kept running. The porch was only a few feet ahead of him. "You miserable little rodent!" called one of the owls. "Did you really think you could sneak away while we were sleeping?"

"Baaad move. Very *very* bad," called another.

"Get him!" called the third. "He's heading for the porch!"

But Ding Dong was too fast for them. He dove under the porch just as the first owl swooped down and snapped at his tail.

"Rats!" screeched the owl.

Ding Dong peeked out from under the porch.

The Fly-by-Nights glared at him from the branch of a tree. "You can't stay there forever," said the first owl.

"Sooner or later you'll have to come out," said the second owl.

"Then we'll get you," said the third owl.

Ding Dong quivered. What if they were right?

Garth in Barbie Land

The sound of a door closing woke Ding Dong out of an exhausted sleep. Two people were walking across the porch above him. His ears shot up. Was it Abigail and one of her parents? They could rescue him!

But it wasn't Abigail. It was someone Ding Dong had never heard before. A boy.

"Why do I have to go and play with her?" he asked. "She's a *girl*, for crying out loud. She'll probably want to play with Barbies or something."

"I'm sure the two of you will find some

common ground," said a woman as she walked down the front steps. "Anyway, she's your age, not an *old* person, right?"

The boy didn't say anything.

"Besides," said the woman, "I could hardly say to her mother, 'Oh, no thanks, never mind, my son hates girls.' "

"I don't hate girls," said the boy. Ding Dong could see his feet as he followed the woman away from the house. "I just don't want to play with them, that's all."

The boy and the woman kept talking. Then a car door slammed shut, and the car drove away. Ding Dong heaved a deep sigh.

He wasn't home. He was under the porch of a stranger's house. And he was stuck there— maybe forever.

Garth and Mrs. Hunter drove slowly around the lake, looking for Cabin 62. Weebie knew better than to ask for the dashboard when Garth's mother was driving. He stayed in Garth's pocket.

"There it is," said Garth.

The cabin looked a lot like the Hunters', except that the windows had flower boxes in them.

As they pulled up, a woman came out and waved. "Hi!" she called. "Come on in. Abigail's inside."

Garth and his mother went into the cabin. The kitchen and living-room walls were covered in knotty pine, just like their house. But the rooms looked bright and cheerful. A kid's drawing of a rabbit hung over the sofa, framed. The girl must have done it, Garth realized.

At that moment she came out of one of the bedrooms.

She was holding a Barbie.

Garth poked an elbow into his mother's side. She shot him The Look.

"Hi," said the girl.

"Hi," said Garth.

Abigail's mother smiled at Mrs. Hunter. "Would you like some coffee?" she asked.

"I'd love some."

Garth and Abigail just stood there looking at each other.

"Why don't you go into Abigail's room?" Abigail's mother said to Garth. "She can show you her stuff."

She turned to Garth's mother. "Abigail isn't in the best shape today, I'm afraid. Losing her rabbit has hit her really hard. She's afraid he'll be . . . hurt . . . out there in the woods."

Garth saw that Abigail's cheeks were wet with tears. He felt bad for her. He knew how he'd feel if he ever lost Weebie.

"Come into my room," said Abigail. Garth followed her.

"Here's my stuff," she said. Garth looked around. There were enough dolls in the room to fill a toy store.

"Uh. Do you have anything else?" he asked her.

She smiled. There was a space between her two front teeth. "Oh, I forgot," she said. "I don't usually play with boys."

"Well, I don't usually play with girls."

They both giggled.

"I have some cards," she offered.

"Great!" said Garth. "Do you know how to play poker?"

"Sure," said Abigail. "My gramps taught me."

"My aunt Barb taught me," said Garth.

They sat on the floor, and Abigail shuffled.

After a minute Garth said, "You miss your rabbit, huh?"

"I'll die if we don't find him," said Abigail.

"That is so sad," Weebie squeaked from Garth's pocket.

"You'll find him," said Garth. "I know you will. I'll look for him. I'll look in the woods around my house."

"Thanks," she said gratefully.

Garth pulled Weebie out of his pocket and set him on the floor. "This is my gerbil," he said to Abigail. "His name is Weebie."

"Aah!" she cried in surprise. Then she bent down to look at him. "He is *so* cute!"

"I am not cute!" Weebie was indignant.

"Is he smart?" she asked.

"Nah," said Garth, just to drive Weebie crazy.

"Oh, but he's so *cute!*" she repeated. "Do you ever dress him up in little clothes and stuff? I bet my Barbie clothes would fit him."

Garth looked horrified. Weebie shrieked.

"I guess boys don't do that," said Abigail.

"Did you do that to your rabbit?" asked Garth.

"Sure," said Abigail. "Barbie's clothes were too small for him, but I had other doll clothes that fit. Dresses and aprons, a flannel nightie. You know.

"I had this one baby bonnet from when I was a baby," she went on, "and my mother let me cut holes in it for his ears. You should have seen him in it—he looked *so* cute! We took pictures—"

"You put a baby bonnet on your *rabbit?*" said Garth.

"No wonder he ran away," said Weebie.

Garth tried to be as gentle as possible. "Do you think he liked it?" he asked Abigail.

It was clear that she hadn't thought much about this before. She started to deal the cards.

"Well," she said slowly, "he did wiggle a lot."

She kept dealing, but she was thinking, too.

"Do you think he hated it?" she asked after a little while.

"I don't know," said Garth softly. "Maybe."

Her eyes filled with tears. "Maybe that's why he ran away!"

"Maybe not," said Garth.

"Absolutely yes!" squeaked Weebie.

"We'll find him, you'll see," Garth assured her.

"If I get him back," said Abigail, "I will never, ever dress him up again."

They played ten games.

Abigail won eight.

An Interesting Discovery

Mr. Hunter was making spaghetti sauce when they got home.

"How'd it go?" he asked Garth.

"It went okay," said Garth. "We played cards."

"They played poker!" squeaked Weebie, sticking his head out of Garth's pocket. Garth pushed him down again.

"Why don't you work on your story until suppertime?" suggested Mr. Hunter. "This sauce takes a while."

"Okay," said Garth. He had decided to try some writing while he was on vacation. He was working on a story about invaders from the planet Sploodge. They killed everybody with incredibly powerful death rays.

Garth was having trouble. He was up to the middle of the story, and the Sploodgians had killed everybody. Now he didn't know how to end it.

He found his spiral notebook and his blue felt-tip pen and sat down at the table. Weebie scurried around, inspecting the salt and pepper shakers and hunting for cookie crumbs.

Garth chewed on his pen and thought. After a while he got an idea. He'd bring everybody back to life. That way there could be a better ending.

He decided to change the story so the Sploodgians didn't really kill everybody; they just put them into a very deep sleep.

Garth crossed out the part about the death rays. He decided that Parker Johnson, the kid hero, would wake up and get rid of the Sploodgians. He wasn't sure how, though.

He glanced out the window. The sun was setting and the sky looked really nice. "Let's go out on the porch, Weeb," he said, gathering up his notebook and his pen.

They went outside. Garth settled on the porch steps and put Weebie down beside him. Then he started writing again. It wasn't long before he got a *really* good idea. Parker found out that the Sploodgians couldn't stand to hear the word "cute." It made them so nauseous that they fell down and gagged and retched.

"You're *SO CUTE!*" Parker told them, in a really loud, cheerful voice—

"Um . . ."

Garth looked up. "Did you say 'Um'?" he asked Weebie.

"No, I did not say 'Um,' " replied Weebie.

"Ahem . . ."

"Weebie, did you say 'Ahem'?" asked Garth.

"I have never said 'Ahem' in my life," Weebie told him. He started looking around the porch. He scampered over to the front, craning his neck over the edge.

"Hey!" he squeaked. "Somebody's down there!"

"Really?"

Weebie peered under the porch. "It's a bunny!" he announced. "Wait a second. It's a *white* bunny!"

"Abigail's bunny!" cried Garth. He scrambled down the steps and lay down on his stomach so he could see under the porch. There was the bunny, with a very dirty, bedraggled blue bow around his neck.

"Hi," said the bunny timidly.

"Ding Dong? Are you Ding Dong?" asked Garth.

"That's me."

"Well, come on out of there! We need to take you home. Abigail's really worried about you."

"Yeah, she's crying and everything," said Weebie.

"Um . . . I can't come out," said Ding Dong.

"Why not?" asked Garth.

"See them?" said Ding Dong, indicating the Fly-by-Nights, who were up on a branch nearby. "They'll eat me as soon as I come out. They're after me."

"They're sleeping," said Garth, looking at the three birds.

"They'll wake up any second," said Ding Dong. "It's almost night."

"Hmmm . . ." Garth tried to figure out what to do.

"Hey! How come you can talk to me?" asked the bunny.

"It's a long story," said Garth. "I just can, that's all."

"I'll bet you're hungry," said Weebie. "How long have you been under there, anyhow?"

"Since this morning," said Ding Dong. "But I haven't eaten anything since yesterday."

Garth jumped up. "I'll get you some food," he said. "Wait here."

"I'm not going anywhere," said Ding Dong.

"Garth!" said Weebie. "Don't leave me here. What if the owls wake up? Put me in your pocket!"

"Good point," said Garth, scooping Weebie up.

A few minutes later they were back with

some carrots and spinach leaves. When Garth put them under the porch, Ding Dong lunged for them.

"Oh!" he exclaimed with his mouth full. "This is wonderful. Wonderful!"

"But not as wonderful as you're going to taste," said a voice from above. Garth, Weebie, and Ding Dong jumped. Then they looked up.

The owls were awake.

A Taste Treat for the Fly-by-Nights

"**O**kay, bunny," snapped the first owl. "Say your prayers."

Garth scrambled to his feet. "Hey, wait a second," he said. "You can't have this bunny. I'm protecting him."

"Protecting him, my tail feathers," said the first owl. "He's ours."

"He's mine," insisted Garth.

"We'll see about that," said the owl darkly.

Weebie had burrowed down as far as he could into Garth's pocket. He wasn't saying a word.

"This is our territory," said the owl, "not yours. And here's what you have to understand: Life goes on in a certain way in these woods. Bunnies eat leaves. Owls eat bunnies. That's just the way it is."

Garth thought about this. Everybody had to eat, even owls. There was no denying it.

But he had to save Ding Dong. How could he do it?

"Let me ask you a question," he said to the first owl. "What if I gave you something to eat that was even better than a bunny? Would you leave the bunny alone?"

"Better than a bunny?" said the second owl. "There is nothing better than a bunny."

"Just give it a try," said Garth.

The Fly-by-Nights had a conference. "All right," said the first owl. "We have nothing to lose."

"If we like what you have, we'll leave the bunny alone," said the second owl.

"If we don't, we eat the bunny," said the third owl.

Garth got up. "We'll see about that last part," he said.

"Wait!" said the first owl, cocking his head. Then the other owls did it, too. They seemed to be sniffing the air.

"I'll tell you what," said the first owl, not quite looking into Garth's eyes. "You can keep the rabbit."

"I can?" said Garth.

"Yeah. All you have to do is give us whatever's in your pocket."

Garth felt Weebie jump as if he'd been given an electric shock. He put his hand over his pocket protectively.

"No way," said Garth. "We had a deal."

"Okay, okay," said the owl. "But whatever it is, it sure smells tasty."

Weebie curled himself into a ball the size of a vitamin pill. Garth had never felt him get so tiny.

"Don't worry, Weeb," he said. "I'll never let them get you. Besides, I have an idea. I think it might work."

He went into the kitchen and started looking around in the cupboard.

"What are you looking for?" asked his father, who was making a salad.

"Uh—nothing," said Garth. He kept looking.

"Well, whatever that nothing is," said Mr. Hunter, "don't ruin your appetite with it. Dinner's almost ready."

"I won't, I promise," said Garth.

Ah. There it was, on the top shelf: the Mallomars box. He lifted it out quietly and did a sideways exit from the kitchen so his father wouldn't see it.

On the porch he ripped the box open. "You're really going to like these," he told the owls. "No joke." He took three Mallomars out of the box and set them on the ground side by side. "Try them," he said.

The owls eyed the cookies with suspicion.

"They don't move," said the first owl.

"They don't smell like much," said the second.

"Just try them," said Garth.

The Fly-by-Nights swooped down together and picked up one cookie each. Then they took them back up to their tree and tore into them.

"Hey," said the first. "This is good."

"This is great," said the second.

"Way better than bunnies," agreed the third.

In seconds all three Mallomars were gone.

Success! Garth was elated. "I'll tell you what," he said to the owls. "You can have the whole box if you take it away and don't come back."

"Deal," said the first owl quickly.

"But boss," said the second owl, "how do we get more of this stuff?"

"You can't," said Garth. "Not unless you hold up a grocery store."

"We'll just have to go back to little furry things," said the third owl sadly.

Garth put the box of Mallomars down on the ground and stepped back. With a rush of its great wings the first owl swooped down and

took up the box in his beak. Then he flew off, with the other owls following him.

Garth waited a few minutes to make sure the owls weren't coming back. Then he crouched down beside the porch. "You can come out now," he told Ding Dong. "It's safe."

"Are you *sure*?"

"I'm sure. They're gone."

"I'm not coming out of your pocket, though," said Weebie. "Not until we're inside."

Garth picked up Ding Dong and carried him into the house.

"Look who I found," he announced.

"Abigail's missing bunny!" cried his mother.

"Where did you find him?" asked his father.

Garth told them that the bunny had been under the porch.

"Gee, I'll bet the poor little guy's been scared," said his mother. She took Ding Dong from Garth and patted his head.

"I think you're right, Mom," said Garth. He picked up the phone and dialed.

"Hi, Abigail," he said. "It's Garth. I have some really good news for you."

Abigail's Promise

As they drove over to Abigail's cabin, Garth sat in the back with Ding Dong on his lap and Weebie in his pocket. Garth couldn't talk to them because his parents were up front. That didn't stop Ding Dong and Weebie from chatting, though.

"Those owls are so *scary!*" said Ding Dong.

"Oh, they're not so bad," said Weebie, from the safety of Garth's pocket. "Their bark is worse than their bite."

"You're crazy, gerbil," said Ding Dong. He shuddered as he remembered his time out in the woods. Those wild-rabbit cousins of his could dance and thump and chant all they liked. They still had to hide from birds like the Fly-by-Nights.

They pulled up to Abigail's cabin, and Abigail flew down the steps with a huge smile on her face. Ding Dong was glad to see her. The car stopped, and she scooped him up as soon as Garth opened the door.

"Oh, Ding Dong!" she said, burying her face in his fur. "I'm so happy to see you. And I will never, ever dress you up in doll clothes again. I promise!"

"Hey! Great!" said Ding Dong.

"Way to go, Ding!" squeaked Weebie.

While the parents chatted in the living room, Abigail and Garth took the animals into her room, where she made a big fuss over Ding Dong. She hugged him, fed him carrots and pea pods, and best of all took the blue ribbon from around his neck and threw it away.

Not long after, Abigail's mother stuck her head in the door. "We're all going to have

supper together," she said. "Your parents have invited us over, Garth."

"Cool," said Garth.

"Can I bring Ding Dong?" asked Abigail.

"As long as there are no owls," said Ding Dong a little nervously.

"Sure," said Abigail's mother.

The meal was fun. Mr. Hunter's spaghetti sauce was a big success, and the parents had a good time talking about food, and the country store, and real estate. After supper Abigail and Garth played Monopoly. Weebie and Ding Dong kept telling Garth to buy hotels, but he ignored them. He wasn't ready to talk to them in front of anybody yet. Nice as Abigail was, she'd probably think he was hallucinating or something.

So she bought all the hotels, and he lost.

Later that night, when the two families were saying good-bye, they decided to go hiking at Acadia National Park the next day.

"This is really nice," Abigail's mother said to Mrs. Hunter. "Abigail was so lonesome. Now she's got her rabbit *and* a friend."

"It's nice for Garth, too," said Mrs. Hunter.

And it was. Abigail was pretty okay, for a girl.

After everyone left, Garth stayed outside on the porch with Weebie. The stars were beautiful.

Garth was startled out of his dreamy state by a strange sound—almost like a belch—from above.

He looked up. The Fly-by-Nights were perched in a tree nearby, swaying slightly.

"Oooh, my stomach," said the first owl. "What were those brown things, anyway? I think I ate too many of them."

"Me too," said the second owl.

"Me three," said the third.

"Whoooo who-who-whoooo-YEARGHHH!" they all moaned together. Weebie, who had scampered into Garth's pocket as soon as he heard them, snickered.

"A deal's a deal," said Garth as he went back into the house.

* * *

The rest of Garth's vacation went quickly. He and Abigail played knock-hockey together, and he read her some of his story. By the time he left, he had almost convinced her to change Ding Dong's name to Ace.

On the last day the Hunters packed up, cleaned the house, and locked the door behind them. Mr. Hunter put the key back under the flowerpots.

"We'd better get going," he said. "We have to pick up Joan before eight."

Since it was daytime, the ride home was a lot better than the ride up. Garth and his mother played a long game of geography, which he almost won with Weebie's help.

Hours later they pulled up at Pet Paradise. Everyone trooped in to get Joan.

She was brushed and fluffed, all ready to be picked up. The lady in pink put her into her carrier along with a catnip toy. While his parents settled the bill, Garth carried her out to the car.

"So how was it?" he asked, once they were in the backseat.

"It was okay."

"Just okay?" he asked. "Did you do anything nice?"

"I guess so. I made friends with a Siamese named Bruce. His place was next door."

But Joan's tone of voice wasn't quite right. She sounded distant. As if her feelings were hurt.

"Is something wrong?" Garth asked her.

"Well," she said, "I was sort of hoping for a postcard."